The Party Fairies

To Charlotte Ingle, a real fashion fairy, with love

Special thanks to
Sue Mongredien

ORCHARD BOOKS

First published in Great Britain in 2005 by Orchard Books
This edition published in 2016 by The Watts Publishing Group

1 3 5 7 9 10 8 6 4 2

© 2016 Rainbow Magic Limited.
© 2016 HIT Entertainment Limited.
Illustrations © Georgie Ripper 2005

HiT entertainment

A CIP catalogue record for this book is available from the British Library.

ISBN 978 1 40834 870 3

Printed in Great Britain

MIX
Paper from
responsible sources
FSC
www.fsc.org
FSC® C104740

The paper and board used in this book are made from wood from responsible sources

Orchard Books
An imprint of Hachette Children's Group
Part of The Watts Publishing Group Limited
Carmelite House, 50 Victoria Embankment, London EC4Y 0DZ

An Hachette UK Company
www.hachette.co.uk
www.hachettechildrens.co.uk

Phoebe
the Fashion
Fairy

by Daisy Meadows

illustrated by Georgie Ripper

Join the Rainbow Magic Reading Challenge!

Read the story and collect your fairy points to climb the Reading Rainbow online. Turn to the back of the book for details!

This book is worth 5 points.

A Very Special Party Invitation

Our gracious King and gentle Queen
Are loved by fairies all.
One thousand years have they ruled well,
Through troubles great and small.

In honour of their glorious reign
A party has been planned,
To celebrate their jubilee
Throughout all Fairyland.

The party is a royal surprise,
We hope they'll be delighted.
So shine your wand and press your dress...
For you have been invited!

RSVP: HRH THE FAIRY GODMOTHER

Contents

Birthday Trouble

Kirsty Tate and Rachel Walker
were busy wrapping a birthday
present for Kirsty's friend, Charlotte.

"There," said Kirsty, tying the
ribbon. "Charlotte's going to love
this silver hairband, it's so pretty."

"Are you nearly ready, girls?"
Mrs Tate called up the stairs.

"Dad and I have to leave in two minutes!"

"Just coming, Mum," Kirsty replied. Then she turned to Rachel. "I can't believe we're going to another party, can you?" she grinned.

Rachel shook her head. "I wonder what's going to happen this time," she said excitedly.

The two girls shared a secret. They were friends with the fairies! And while Rachel had been staying with Kirsty's family, the girls had been helping the Party Fairies of Fairyland.

Grumpy Jack Frost had sent his goblin servants into the world to cause trouble at human parties. When a Party Fairy arrived to put things right, a goblin would try to steal her magical party bag and take it back to Jack Frost. Rachel and Kirsty had been helping the fairies keep their party bags safe – which meant that all the parties that week had been extra-specially exciting.

Kirsty and Rachel put their party dresses into a bag with Charlotte's present, then rushed downstairs.

Kirsty's parents had to go out that afternoon, so Mrs Tate had arranged for the girls to go to Charlotte's house a little early.

"We've met nearly all the Party Fairies now," Kirsty said, as she and Rachel walked along the road.

Rachel counted them off on her fingers. "Cherry the Cake Fairy, Melodie the Music Fairy, Grace the Glitter Fairy, Honey the Sweet Fairy and Polly the Party Fun Fairy," she said. "So the only two we haven't met are..."

"Phoebe the Fashion Fairy and Jasmine the Present Fairy," Kirsty put in. "I wonder if we'll see one of them today."

Rachel couldn't help smiling as they walked up Charlotte's front path. "I expect so," she said. "Those goblins won't be able to resist another chance to try and get a magical party bag. One of them is bound to cause trouble, and then Phoebe or Jasmine will have to come and set things right."

The girls knew that Jack Frost had sent his goblins to steal the party bags because he wanted to use fairy magic at a party of his own. It was to rival the Fairy King and Queen's surprise jubilee party, which had been organised by the Fairy Godmother for the end of the week.

Kirsty and Rachel had both been
invited to the jubilee celebrations as
special guests. They were determined to
make sure that Jack Frost and his
goblins didn't spoil everything by
stealing the Party Fairies' party magic.

Kirsty rang the doorbell and a few
moments later, Charlotte answered
the door.

"Happy birthday!"
cried Kirsty and
Rachel together.

But then Kirsty
noticed how sad
her friend was
looking. "Is
everything all
right?" she
asked in concern.

Charlotte didn't seem to be in a birthday mood: she wasn't wearing a party dress and she wasn't even smiling. "No," she wailed. "Everything is *not* all right. My best dress has been ruined!"

"Ruined?" Rachel echoed. "How?"

Charlotte held the front door open. "Come upstairs and see," she said miserably.

Kirsty and Rachel gasped when they saw Charlotte's white and gold party dress hanging on her wardrobe door.

It had messy splodges of what looked like green paint all over it.

"Oh, no!" Kirsty gasped. "How did that happen?"

Charlotte looked close to tears.

"I don't know," she said. "This morning, it was perfectly clean!"

Charlotte's mum, Mrs Ingle, came in. Her mouth fell open when she saw Charlotte's spoiled dress. "Charlotte!" she exclaimed. "You haven't been painting in your best dress, have you?"

"No," Charlotte cried. "I just came upstairs and found it like this!"

Mrs Ingle frowned. "I hope your brother hasn't had anything to do with it," she said, and marched over to open the window. "Will!" she called down the garden. "Come here at once!"

Charlotte's little brother, Will, scampered into the bedroom a few moments later. He was covered in mud and looking very pleased with himself. "I found loads of worms," he told the girls happily, brandishing a small muddy spade.

"Will, your sister's party is starting soon," Mrs Ingle groaned. "You were supposed to be getting ready."

Will glanced over at Charlotte. "Well, Charlotte isn't ready yet — and it's her party!" he protested.

"Speaking of which," Mrs Ingle went on, "do you know anything about this?"

She showed Will Charlotte's party dress and he shook his head vigorously. "I've been in the garden all morning!" he insisted.

Charlotte nodded. "It's true, Mum," she said. "I saw him."

Mrs Ingle sighed. "Well, I suppose the dress must have brushed against something," she said, looking baffled.

Rachel and Kirsty glanced around the room uneasily. They were both wondering if the dress really had brushed against something – or if somebody had ruined it deliberately.

Both girls knew it was just the sort of thing a goblin would do. And the green paint on the dress was an unmistakeable goblin green.

Rachel caught Kirsty's eye and realized that they were both thinking the same thing – a goblin must be hiding somewhere very nearby!

Mrs Ingle looked at her watch. "We've got one hour before the party starts," she said "We could pop round to the dry-cleaner's and see if they can help, but I've still got the fairy cakes to ice. I don't know how I'll get everything done in time."

"We'll ice the cakes for you while you're out," Kirsty suggested cheerfully.

"Yes," Rachel put in. "We're good at icing," she added, remembering the icing they'd made at Kirsty's birthday party.

Mrs Ingle smiled. "That's very kind of you, girls," she said. "Are you sure you wouldn't mind?"

"Of course not. It will be fun," Kirsty replied at once.

Mrs Ingle led the girls downstairs. Then, while Mr Ingle whisked Will away to get him cleaned up, Mrs Ingle took Rachel and Kirsty into the dining room, where the party food had all been laid out on the table. "One tray of fairy cakes, one bowl of icing, a piping bag and some cake decorations," she said, setting them out. "This is really helpful, girls. Thank you!"

Then Charlotte and her
mum hurried off to
the dry-cleaner's
with Charlotte's
ruined dress.

As soon as
Kirsty and Rachel
heard Mrs Ingle's
car leave the driveway,
they looked at each other
meaningfully.

"We've got to find that goblin,"
Kirsty said in a low voice, "before
he does anything else to spoil
the party."

"Well, he must have been in
Charlotte's bedroom not so long ago.
Let's go back up and see if he's still
there," Rachel suggested.

The girls made their way upstairs to Charlotte's room. Kirsty put her finger to her lips, then crept up to the wardrobe and flung the doors wide open.

Rachel's heart was pounding as she and Kirsty peeped inside. Jack Frost's goblins were very sneaky; you could never tell where they were going to pop up.

But there was no sign of the goblin in Charlotte's wardrobe, so Kirsty peered under the bed while Rachel checked behind the curtains.

Then Rachel looked beneath Charlotte's duvet and Kirsty checked on top of all the cupboards.

"Either he's hiding somewhere really, really clever, or he's left the room," Kirsty said at last.

Rachel sighed.
"He could be
anywhere in the
house by now,"
she said. "Just
waiting to cause
more trouble!"

Kirsty glanced
at her watch.
"Come on, we'd
better get on with those
cakes," she said. "Otherwise we'll be
the ones spoiling Charlotte's party."

Downstairs, Kirsty and Rachel began
icing the cakes, trying to think where
the goblin might be hiding. Kirsty piped
heart shapes onto each cake, while
Rachel decorated them with hundreds
and thousands.

Rachel was just finishing the last cake when Kirsty nudged her. "Look!" she urged.

Rachel looked up to see a stream of tiny, sparkly, red hearts floating past the window.

Both girls ran over to take a closer look. There, waving at them through the glass, was a beautiful, smiling fairy!

Goblin Attack

"It's Phoebe the Fashion Fairy!"
Rachel cried, opening the window
for her.

Phoebe had long, wavy blonde
hair, held back by a crimson Alice
band. She wore a little white dress
with a row of red hearts around
the hem and matching shoes.

Her scarlet wand had a ruby
heart at one end that glittered
in the sunlight.

She fluttered inside and perched on
the windowsill. "Hello!" she said in a
bright, silvery voice. "Kirsty and
Rachel, isn't it? I remember seeing you
when Honey the Sweet Fairy showed
you around the Party Fairy workshop."

"That's right," Kirsty said. "And I remember your gorgeous fashion department, with all those wonderful, sparkly fairy dresses."

Phoebe nodded and then looked serious. "Now, I heard that there was a party dress disaster here, so I've come to work a little bit of fairy magic and sort everything out."

"Well, we're very glad to see you," Kirsty said, and quickly filled Phoebe in on what had happened to Charlotte's dress.

Phoebe's delicate features creased into a frown. "That does sound like goblin mischief," she agreed. "We'll have to be careful."

"We'll just clear these icing things away," Rachel said, "and then we'll show you where Charlotte's bedroom is."

Kirsty arranged the fairy cakes on a plate while Rachel started gathering up the icing equipment. Phoebe fluttered over for a closer look at the cakes. "Cherry the Cake Fairy would be proud of you two," she said admiringly, hovering over the table in mid-air.

"These look good enough for the King and Queen of Fairyland themselves!"

Rachel was frowning. "Where's the icing bag?" she asked Kirsty. "I can't see it anywhere."

Kirsty looked round. "It was there a moment ago," she said, pointing to one end of the table.

"I know," Rachel agreed, sounding puzzled. "But it's vanished."

No sooner had she said these words, than the lid of Will's toybox flew back with a loud crash. The girls and Phoebe spun around to see a goblin bursting out of the toy chest like a grinning, green jack-in-the-box.

"It's the goblin!" Kirsty cried.

"With the piping bag!" Rachel added.

The goblin held up the piping bag and squeezed it hard. A jet of icing shot out and hit Phoebe right in the tummy!

"Help!" she cried in surprise, tumbling backwards.

Kirsty and Rachel watched in horror as Phoebe fell. Luckily, she landed in the big, soft, red jelly in the middle of the table and then bounced up into the air again, arms flailing as she tried to recover her balance.

SQUELCH! Back into the jelly, Phoebe plunged. She was quite unhurt, but this time she lost her grip on her magical party bag and it flew across the table.

"Just what I was after," the goblin chortled, leaping out of the toybox.

Rachel gasped. "Oh, no, you don't!" she cried, dashing round the table to try and reach the party bag before the goblin could take it.

But she was too late. And the goblin's gnarly, green hand closed around Phoebe's shimmering party bag, seconds before Rachel could get to it.

The goblin grinned nastily, snatched up a fairy cake in his other hand, and leapt out of the window into the garden.

"Oh, no!" Phoebe gasped, struggling out of the sticky jelly. "I need my party bag or I won't be able to fix Charlotte's dress!"

"And we all know what the goblin
will do with it," Kirsty groaned.
"He'll give it to horrible Jack Frost
for his party."

"We can't let that happen," Phoebe
said firmly, brushing pieces of jelly from
her dress. She waved her wand.
Sparkling red hearts streamed from the
tip and spilled all over Kirsty and
Rachel. "I'll make you fairy-sized," she
said. "Then we can all fly after that
goblin thief."

Kirsty and Rachel shut their eyes in delight as Phoebe's magic got to work and they felt themselves shrinking. Beautiful, shimmering fairy wings appeared on their backs, and Rachel couldn't resist flying a little loop-the-loop. It was so much fun, to be able to fly!

Phoebe fluttered out of the window and the girls followed. They could see the goblin running down the garden, greedily stuffing the fairy cake into his mouth as he went.

He glanced over his shoulder and spotted the three fairies zooming after him. A look of panic crossed his face and he glanced around wildly, searching for somewhere to hide. The next moment he spotted the Wendy House at the bottom of the garden and charged towards it, diving inside and slamming the door.

Phoebe was first to reach the Wendy House. She knocked loudly on the door. "Let me in!" she ordered crossly.

"There's nobody home!" called the goblin from inside.

Phoebe sighed and tried to pull the door open, but the goblin must have been holding tight to the handle on the other side, for it didn't move.

"It's no good, I'm not strong enough," Phoebe wailed.

"If you turn us back into girls, we might be able to do it," Kirsty suggested.

"Good idea," Phoebe said, waving her wand again to release another stream of red hearts.

Kirsty and Rachel felt their arms and legs tingling with fairy magic as they grew back to their normal size.

"Right!" Rachel said, grabbing hold of the door handle. "Let's get this door open."

There was a scraping sound from inside the Wendy House and then, to Rachel's dismay, she found that she couldn't even turn the handle. "The goblin must have wedged something under the door handle," she cried in frustration. "A chair or something – it won't budge at all now!"

Phoebe groaned. "What are we going to do?" she asked anxiously.

Kirsty looked around, desperately trying to think. Seeing the cake crumbs that the goblin had dropped on the grass gave her an idea. Obviously, the goblin liked the cakes she and Rachel had decorated; perhaps they could  tempt him out with some more. She whispered her idea to Phoebe and Rachel, and they both nodded approvingly.

"Goblins always want to get their hands on more cakes," Phoebe laughed, "it's a brilliant idea!" She turned back towards the Ingles' house and waved her wand with an expert flourish.

Kirsty and Rachel watched in delight as a stream of twinkling red hearts shot straight from Phoebe's wand into Charlotte's house. A moment later, something very strange happened...

"Are those what I think they are?" Kirsty asked, staring.

"Flying fairy cakes!" Rachel gasped.

A small procession of cakes was whizzing through the air towards the Wendy House in a neat 'V' formation.

Kirsty's spirits rose as she saw the goblin peering curiously out of one of the Wendy House windows. He licked his lips when he saw the flying cakes.

"He's seen them!" she hissed, crossing her fingers.

The fairy cakes landed neatly on the Wendy House windowsill and then started dancing around, right under the goblin's nose.

"He looks tempted," Rachel whispered, hopefully.

The goblin had his face pressed up against the glass eagerly, but then he caught sight of the girls peeping in at him, and a determined expression came over his face. "If you think I'm coming out for a few measly fairy cakes, you've got another think coming!" he yelled, folding his arms stubbornly. "I know it's a trick and I'm staying here!"

Rachel sighed. She'd been sure the greedy goblin wouldn't be able to resist more cakes. Then she glanced down at her watch and gulped. "Oh, no! We've only got ten minutes before Charlotte's party starts," she cried.

Kirsty looked at her in horror. "Charlotte and her mum will be back any second!" she exclaimed. "We've got to get that goblin out, right now!"

A Wave of Inspiration

Kirsty, Rachel and Phoebe stared around
the garden, wondering what to try next.
Rachel spotted the garden hose and her eyes
lit up as a thought popped into her head.
"How about this?" she asked the other two.
"We put the end of the hose down the
chimney, turn the tap on, and flood that
nasty goblin out of the Wendy House!"

Kirsty chuckled. "I love it!" she said.

Phoebe was smiling, too. "Goblins don't like water, and they hate getting cold, wet feet," she added. "If anything's going to get him out of there, a cold shower will."

Quickly, Kirsty dangled the end of the hosepipe down the Wendy House

chimney, while Rachel ran to turn on the outside tap. A few moments later, there came a great *SPLASH!* – quickly followed by a surprised yelp from the goblin.

"Where's that rain coming from?" he grumbled. "I'm getting wet."

"Come out, then," Phoebe called. "It's lovely and dry out here!"

More water splashed into the Wendy House and the goblin's moans got louder. "Now my feet are wet," he groaned. "Ugh, horrible cold water. Make it stop!"

"We'll make it stop, if you come out

and give Phoebe her party bag," Kirsty offered. "Shan't!" the goblin retorted rudely. "This party bag is mine now, and I'm going to give it to Jack Frost!"

"Well, you can't say we didn't warn you, goblin," Rachel shouted, racing over to turn the tap on fully. "Here comes the flood!"

Water poured into the Wendy
House in torrents. Through the
window, the girls and Phoebe could
see the goblin bobbing helplessly
around as the water level rose.

Then he floated against the small
chair he'd used to wedge the door
shut. The chair was knocked aside
and the Wendy House door flew open.

"Help!" cried the goblin, as a huge wave of water gushed out of the Wendy House door, carrying him along on top of it.

"I didn't know goblins could surf!" Kirsty laughed as he sailed past her. She stretched out an arm and snatched Phoebe's party bag from his hands. "Got it!" she declared

happily, passing the bag to
Phoebe.

The goblin shrieked and flapped
about in the river of water, trying
to get to his feet. But it was
impossible, the rushing stream
carried him all the way down the
garden to the pond. *SPLOSH!*
Into the pond went the goblin.

Kirsty, Rachel and Phoebe couldn't help laughing as they watched the goblin clamber out, dripping wet and with a huge clump of duckweed plastered to his head. He looked very sorry for himself.

"I'm almost tempted to magic him a special outfit," Phoebe chuckled. "Some swimming trunks, goggles and a nice, flowery swimming hat!"

SQUELCH, SQUELCH, SQUELCH!

The goblin stomped away, defeated.

"I think that's the last we'll see of
our soggy friend today," Kirsty said
with a grin.

Rachel ran to turn the tap off, and
then waved frantically at
Phoebe and Kirsty.
"Mrs Ingle's back
with Charlotte!"
she hissed.
"I just heard
the car!"

Kirsty's face fell.
Not only was the
garden a mud-bath
now, but the Wendy House was
a mess, the big, red jelly was ruined,
and she and Rachel were all wet, too!
How on earth were they going to
explain everything to Mrs Ingle?

"Leave it to me," Phoebe said quickly. "You keep Charlotte's mum talking. I'll fix the Wendy House and then the dining room. Now, hurry!"

Kirsty and Rachel ran into the house to find poor Charlotte looking more upset than ever. "The cleaners said they'd never seen anything like this paint," she explained sadly. "They tried all sorts of things to get it off my dress but nothing would shift it."

Mrs Ingle put a comforting arm around her daughter. "Never mind," she said. "You've got lots of other nice things to wear. You'll just have to choose something else."

She glanced over at Kirsty and Rachel, as Charlotte began to trudge upstairs. "And you two should change, too," Mrs Ingle went on. "The party's going to start any minute." A puzzled frown appeared between her eyebrows as she took in Rachel and Kirsty's damp clothes. "You look rather wet. Are you all right?" she asked.

"Um..." Kirsty began, not sure how to explain her bedraggled appearance.

"We're fine," Rachel put in hastily. "We just got a bit splashed when we were washing up the icing things, that's all."

Mrs Ingle's frown cleared. "I'd completely forgotten about the fairy cakes," she said. "Did you get them all finished?" She walked towards the dining room door.

"Well, we, er..." Rachel mumbled, crossing her fingers as she followed Mrs Ingle into the room.

Could Phoebe possibly have had time to magic the Wendy House back to normal *and* sort out the dining room?

A Dress to Impress

Kirsty and Rachel shouldn't have worried; clever Phoebe had worked wonders! The fairy cakes were neatly arranged on their plate once more, and the jelly was its perfect wobbly self again; nobody would ever dream that a Party Fairy had fallen into it just twenty minutes ago.

Kirsty blinked as she noticed a tiny glimmer of sparkly red light flicker around the table, then vanish quickly. She turned to Rachel questioningly, and Rachel nodded. She had seen it, too. A last sparkle of fairy magic!

Luckily, Mrs Ingle had noticed no such thing: she was too busy admiring the fairy cakes. "You are clever, girls," she said. "I couldn't have decorated them more beautifully myself – thank you so much."

"You're welcome," Kirsty said, smiling with relief. "Now, we'd better go and get changed."

Just then, there was an excited cry from upstairs. "Kirsty, Rachel! Come quickly!"

Kirsty and Rachel rushed up to Charlotte's room. To their amazement, hanging on the wardrobe door, were three gorgeous party dresses. One was a beautiful deep red, all covered in golden hearts, with a matching hairband. A tag hanging from the sleeve said 'Charlotte' in pretty, sparkly writing.

The other two dresses had tags that read 'Kirsty' and 'Rachel'. Kirsty's dress was pink with a lilac dragonfly embroidered near the hem, and Rachel's dress was lilac with pink butterflies around the neckline.

"This is the most beautiful dress ever," Charlotte breathed, stroking the shimmering red material. "But where did it come from?"

Rachel opened her mouth but couldn't think of a single thing to say. How could they explain that the three outfits were fairy gifts, created by Phoebe the Fashion Fairy?

"Happy birthday, Charlotte!" Kirsty cried, thinking quickly. "It's our present to you. We, er, went and got it while you were out – just in case the cleaners couldn't fix your dress."

"And here's a little something else, as well," Rachel added, pulling the present they'd wrapped up earlier out of the bag. "Happy birthday!"

"Oh, thank you!" Charlotte cried happily, hugging both girls.

As Charlotte started opening the present, Kirsty suddenly nudged Rachel.

Rachel turned to see what her friend had spotted. To her delight, the dragonfly and butterflies on their party dresses were fluttering their delicate embroidered wings and twinkling with golden lights. She grinned at Kirsty – they were both going to be wearing magical dresses!

Charlotte was pulling off the last bit of wrapping paper. "What a gorgeous necklace!" she exclaimed, holding it up. "I love it."

Kirsty and Rachel stared. The silver hairband they'd wrapped up for Charlotte back at Kirsty's house had been turned into a gleaming golden necklace with three, heart-shaped red beads strung in the middle.

Phoebe's work again, no doubt, Kirsty thought, smiling.

Charlotte pulled on her dress and Rachel fastened the necklace around her neck.

"I must go and show Mum," Charlotte said, twirling around happily.

"Thank you so much. This is turning out to be the best birthday I've ever had!"

As soon as Charlotte had left the room, Phoebe peeped out from behind a curtain. With a smile, she waved her wand, and Kirsty and Rachel suddenly found themselves wearing their new party dresses, while their old clothes were neatly folded in piles on the bed.

"Oh, Phoebe, these dresses are just gorgeous," Kirsty declared, standing in front of the mirror. "Thank you!"

"I feel like a fairy all over again, wearing this," Rachel added, dancing around in her new dress.

Phoebe's cheeks blushed pink. "Oh, it's nothing," she said, looking terribly pleased. "I'm just doing my job. Happy to help!" Then she smiled. "Anyway, I should be thanking you for saving my party bag from the goblin."

"Oh, it's nothing," Kirsty grinned.

"Happy to help," Rachel laughed.

"Just doing our job!" they chorused.

Phoebe came over and hugged them.

"Have a lovely party," she said. "I must fly back to Fairyland now."

Kirsty and Rachel waved goodbye as Phoebe disappeared in a swirl of glittering fairy dust.

Then the doorbell rang downstairs. "Charlotte's friends are here," Kirsty said happily. "Let's go and have some fun. I think we've earned it today."

"We certainly have," Rachel agreed. "And I can't wait for our next adventure!"

**Now Rachel and Kirsty
must help...**

Jasmine the Present Fairy

Read on for a sneak peek...

"Look at all these stalls, Rachel," Kirsty Tate said, pointing down the street where she lived. "This is going to be a great party!"

All of Kirsty's neighbours were bustling around setting up stalls outside their houses. There were all sorts of things going on, from games and raffles to stalls selling bric-a-brac and cakes. Delicious smells wafted towards the girls, from the barbecue at the other end of the street. The road was closed to traffic, and people were already milling around in the sunshine, enjoying the fête.

"I think having a street party is a great idea," Rachel Walker, Kirsty's best friend, said with a grin. "I wish we had one in our street back home." Rachel had come to stay with Kirsty for a week of the Easter holidays.

Kirsty was opening the last box of books. "We'd better hurry and put these on the stall," she said. "Lots of people are arriving now."

"I'm glad the party is today, before I go home tomorrow," Rachel said, helping Kirsty arrange the books on the stall that Mr and Mrs Tate were running. "I hope we raise loads of money for charity."

"We always do," said Kirsty happily,

stacking the books neatly. "Lots of people come to the party from all over town. But..." she lowered her voice, "...we'll have to be extra-careful this year, won't we?"

Rachel nodded solemnly. "Yes," she agreed. "A party means we must keep our eyes open for goblin mischief!"

Rachel and Kirsty shared a wonderful secret. They had become friends with the fairies and now, whenever their fairy friends were in trouble, Rachel and Kirsty were happy to help. The cause of the trouble was usually cold, spiky Jack Frost, who had been banished to his ice castle by the King and Queen of Fairyland...

Read Jasmine the Present Fairy
to find out what adventures are in store for Kirsty and Rachel!

Meet the
Friendship Fairies

When Jack Frost steals the Friendship Fairies' magical objects, BFFs everywhere are in trouble! Can Rachel and Kirsty help save the magic of friendship?

www.rainbowmagicbooks.co.uk

Calling all parents, carers and teachers!
The Rainbow Magic fairies are here to help
your child enter the magical world of reading.
Whatever reading stage they are at, there's
a Rainbow Magic book for everyone!
Here is Lydia the Reading Fairy's guide to
supporting your child's journey at all levels.

Starting Out

Our Rainbow Magic Beginner Readers are perfect for first-time readers who are just beginning to develop reading skills and confidence. Approved by teachers, they contain a full range of educational levelling, as well as lively full-colour illustrations.

Developing Readers

Rainbow Magic Early Readers contain longer stories and wider vocabulary for building stamina and growing confidence. These are adaptations of our most popular Rainbow Magic stories, specially developed for younger readers in conjunction with an Early Years reading consultant, with full-colour illustrations.

Going Solo

The Rainbow Magic chapter books – a mixture of series and one-off specials – contain accessible writing to encourage your child to venture into reading independently. These highly collectible and much-loved magical stories inspire a love of reading to last a lifetime.

www.rainbowmagicbooks.co.uk

"Rainbow Magic got my daughter reading chapter books. Great sparkly covers, cute fairies and traditional stories full of magic that she found impossible to put down" - Mother of Edie (6 years)

"Florence LOVES the Rainbow Magic books. She really enjoys reading now" Mother of Florence (6 years)

The Rainbow Magic Reading Challenge

Well done, fairy friend – you have completed the book!
This book was worth 5 points.

See how far you have climbed on the **Reading Rainbow**
on the Rainbow Magic website below.

The more books you read, the more points you will get,
and the closer you will be to becoming a Fairy Princess!

How to get your Reading Rainbow
1. Cut out the coin below
2. Go to the Rainbow Magic website
3. Download and print out your poster
4. Add your coin and climb up the Reading Rainbow!

There's all this and lots more at
www.rainbowmagicbooks.co.uk

You'll find activities, competitions, stories, a special
newsletter and complete profiles of all the
Rainbow Magic fairies. Find a fairy with your name!